# Inspire To Act *for Kids*

## Jennifer A. Borislow
## Mark S. Gaunya

STRATEGIC VISION
PUBLISHING

Strategic Vision Publishing
1 Griffin Brook Drive
Methuen, MA 01844

www.strategicvisionpublishing.com

ISBN: 978-0-9825459-3-5

# Introduction

Teachers have a profound and lasting impact on the lives of children. When you think about it, we are all teachers in one way or another. We are parents, caregivers, and friends providing encouragement, inspiration and valuable guidance to children. One undeniable truth is children model others and at that time, they don't really see how their behavior can affect others- whether in a kind and gentle way or in a mean way. Kindness is a value that can be taught and modeled from the basic level of teaching a child to say please and thank you or reminding them to follow the "Golden Rule" and only speak kindly of others.

Kindness has no age restriction. It is the connection that links us all together and strengthens the bonds of our communities, neighborhoods and families. Once they are taught how, simple acts of kindness are natural to children. They are often unaware how easily they can brighten someone's day. Children have an innocence that allows them to be interested, engaged, inquisitive, thoughtful and carefree. They feel good about themselves when they help others and receive praise for their good deeds. Great parents and teachers understand the importance of teaching values and nurturing love. The world can seem like a frightening place to a child but an extended hand of kindness can make it a much better place to live.

Inspiring others to act with kindness begins with doing for others. In can be as simple as a smile, a hug or a helping hand. Positive connections have a direct impact of how we feel about ourselves and how children interact with others. The stories in this book are simple and yet very powerful. They illustrate the ease in which children think of others.

We hope that you will enjoy the short stories inspired by kids. May the words and actions of these children touch your heart, enrich your soul and inspire you to act.

# Stories from the Heart at Home

Maeve, age 13

# Something Sweet, Something Sour

A few summers ago, when I was in 6th grade, 3 of my friends and I started a lemonade stand to raise money for leukemia, a form of blood cancer commonly found in young children. We sold lemonade, desserts, and even bracelets that we made. We hung up posters around our town spreading the word, and invited people from our school to stop by. Many people appreciated the cause and donated without even buying anything. We ended up raising a few hundred dollars that we sent to the Leukemia and Lymphoma Society. We got a letter of thanks from the Society, and it felt great to know we had helped people going through a painful time.

*Maeve, age 13*

Valerie, age 6

# Front Door Surprise

My two sisters and I decided to head to the mall and put together three care packages. We included things like gum, hair bows, lip gloss, phone cases, candy, skin care items and other small goodies. We purchased 3 blank cards along with 3 bags and tissue paper. We then went home and put together our packages and cards just telling the recipient to have a good day and that someone is thinking about them. We also typed up a letter to attach to each bag explaining that we hoped these people would pass on these acts by anonymously doing something for someone else. That night we left these packages on the doorsteps of girls who we knew who could use some kindness. The feeling of doing something kind for someone else is always the best feeling and I'm so glad I got to do it with my sisters.

*Sarah, age 10*

# The Birthday Girl

I didn't want presents for my 8th birthday. Instead I wanted to celebrate with my grandma who is living in a home with other grandmas. My grandma just got out of the hospital and was sad that she was going to miss my birthday party. So, we had my birthday at grandmas new place and had cake and ice cream and played some games and sang songs. Instead of presents, I asked my friends to bring puzzles, books, yarn and knitting needles so we could give them to the other grandmas. My mom helped me come up with the idea and it was so much fun to see my grandma happy.

*Chelsea, age 8*

## Homework Help

Every night my mom and I sit down at the kitchen table and do our homework.   We do it together because I help my mom with hers.  My mom does not speak English well, so I translate the work for her.  It is something we can do together which is always fun!

*Angelina, age 6*

## Swinging to the Rescue

I have a younger brother. He has trouble swinging by himself; he needs a little push. We went into the backyard and I pushed him on the swing. He was really happy and so was I!

*Nathaniel, age 6*

## Snowy Surprise

There has been so much snow this year; which makes building snow castles so much fun. I took a break from building castles and helped my mom shovel. We shoveled so much snow! It was fun helping my mom and I know she was happy that I helped.

*Valerie, age 6*

Makenna, age 8

# A BIG Fan

I love to play hockey and next year I can play on a team. My favorite hockey team is the Boston Bruins and my favorite player is Reilly Smith. I saved my money to buy a ticket and then my mom and I got to go on a train to see my first Bruins game on New Year's Eve. It was very exciting even though they lost in a shoot-out. I had fun. The nice lady in front of me bought me some Bruins stuff- a hat, a Smith t-shirt and a hockey stick and puck. I decided to share with my baby brother. He couldn't come to the game so I gave him the hockey stick and puck and I kept the hat and shirt. He was very happy.

*Vincent, age 8*

# The Lawn Guys

Every week the lawn people show up at our house to mow our lawn. My father used to cut the lawn but now he has the lawn people. They are nice guys and I like to hang outside to see them. They say, "Hello" and talk to me. They know my name. They are very friendly and sometimes I get to ride with them on the mower. When it is hot outside- I bring them water and sometimes my mother bakes them brownies. Someday I will be able to help them mow the lawn.

*Trevor, age 5*

# The Guardian Angel

Last year my Nana died and my mother was very sad. She cried a lot and some days she didn't even leave the house. My dad said that my mother was missing Nana and that is why she was so sad. I tried to make her laugh and be happy. I miss my Nana but my mom misses her more. My dad and I bought my mother an angel ornament for Christmas to remind her that Nana was in heaven and that she was a guardian angel looking out for all of us. That made my mother cry again but this time it was happy tears. She is still sad some days but she can look at the guardian angel and know that nana is watching over us.

*Ellie, age 9*

Maeve, age 13

# Blossoming

Yesterday I bought my mom flowers. She is always buying me toys. She takes care of me and my sisters and doesn't ask for anything in return. So I decided to buy her flowers with my dad. When I gave them to her she smiled and gave me a big hug. She also told me she loved me and that I had no idea how much it meant to her. It made me feel good to know I did something to make her happy because I know she would do anything for me. I will most definitely do something else kind for her in the future to show how much I love and appreciate her hard work.

*Timmy, age 10*

Kiley, age 6

# Chalk Talk

I decided that my dad needed a special thank you from his loving daughters. He is always up to playing with us, and reading us books, even after he has had a long day at work. My sister and I like to write and draw in our driveway and on the street with chalk. One day before he got home from work, we grabbed our sidewalk chalk and went to work writing on the end of our driveway. We drew hearts, and flowers and a BIG sign that said "We Love you! Thank you for being the best Dad! We even drew a picture of the three of us. When my dad came home from work and saw what we had drawn he had a BIG smile on his face!

*Hannah, age 9*

*Maeve, age 13*

# One less Worry

Whenever my mom and I go shopping, we always have a great time; Even if we are just at the grocery store. Every single week I always make sure to carry in and put away the groceries with my mom. She has 3 kids, including me, so sometimes she has to do many things at once. Putting away the groceries means that she has one less thing to worry about each week and I know it makes a difference to her. Because my mom always provides for me and my siblings I feel like me putting everything away is no big deal and it makes a difference to my mom!

Sophia, age 12

# Giving Jar

We started a "giving jar" at our house where we collect loose change we find or that mom finds in the laundry, or we can do things around the house to earn money to put into the jar. Then once the jar is full we take the money we have collected and use it to do random acts of kindness. We have paid for breakfast/coffee for the person behind us in line at the donut store, we have bought flowers to give to a stranger, and we have even used it to buy canned goods and other items to donate to our local pantry. Every time we empty the jar we can't wait to start saving again for our next adventures.

*Zack, age 7*

# All You Need Is Change

Often times my dad comes home from work and gives me the change he has in his pockets. I have been collecting the change in a big jar in my bedroom. One day my teacher talked about bringing in old books to give to kids who don't have books. I came up with an idea to collect loose change from other kids. We put a big water jug in the classroom and for 6 weeks all the kids brought in loose change and put it in the water jug. We collected almost $66 and bought 50 new books for kids.

*Nicolas, age 7*

# Spreading Extra Warmth

My brother and I went through all of our old coats and winter stuff. We had so much extra we donated things that didn't fit us to the local shelter. We wanted to make sure kids that did not have a coat would get one this year!

*Eliza, age 8*

# A Friendly Visitor

For years, I have lived next door to an elderly woman who is 93 years old. She lives by herself. She has trouble hearing and wears a hearing aid and just recently lost her driver's license because she is not able to see very well. She doesn't come out of her house too often so my mom cooks extra food at dinner time and I take it over to her. I also help her shovel the driveway in the winter and rake leaves in the fall. She doesn't have many visitors and told me I brighten up her day when I go over to her house. Sometimes I sit on her back deck and have ice cream with her. She likes that! She is a very kind lady and I am happy to be her friend.

*Jessica, age 10*

# Big Brother

My mom always works hard for me and my sisters. One day she needed to go to the grocery store but didn't want to leave my little sister home alone. I watched my little sister while my mom was out of the house for the first time that day. My little sister and I ended up having a lot of fun and my mom appreciated it. It was not very hard and I would be willing to do it again one day.

*Brendan, age 12*

# Kindness in Bloom

We have a garden in our backyard. Last spring my mom let me have my own corner and grow tulips. I was so excited! My mom showed me how to plant the bulbs and watch them grow! When they were fully bloomed, I picked them. I created a bouquet of tulips for my mom as a thank you for showing me how to garden. Now every time the flowers bloom, I create a bouquet and give it to a neighbor, teacher or my bus driver as a way to show appreciation.

*Ginger, age 7*

# Stories Helping the Community

# Handle With Care

In my church we have two men that are pilots in the military. They are both overseas on a tour of duty and will not be home for Christmas. Each Sunday we pray for their safety and their family who worries about them.    My Sunday school teacher suggested we should send them a Christmas care package so we asked their moms what they needed. They told us that they need simple things like, gum, cough drops, Chap Stick, pocket size Kleenex and beef jerky. I took the list and my mom and I went shopping and we bought a lot of the stuff for their care packages. We collected so much stuff that we made extra care packages to give to their friends. We hope they will like our surprise!!

*Hanson, age 7*

# A Bite to Eat and a Bag of Treats

I was at my family's shop in Haverhill. I noticed a homeless man had come into our store, he seemed very hungry. My first interaction with the man was a surprising one. He was filled with jokes. First I fetched some soup we had in our storage. I gave him the soup along with some crackers. The look on his face was so bright and joyful. As he was enjoying the soup, I was going around my shop to collect some things he could use. I got some bottled water, crackers, matches, bags of chips, cookies and a loaf of bread. I paid my father for all the items. As he was ready to leave I handed him the bag full of food and other necessities. He shed a tear right as he opened the bag and was even happier than before. Charlie was very thankful to me and my father. He gave me a really big hug and said, "Thank You".

*Prit, age 12*

# Every Little Bit Counts

One time, my mom, sister and I were on our way to Boston. As we were entering Boston, we noticed two homeless men directing traffic. My mom mentioned how she always sees them doing this and just having a good time. I had the idea to give him money, so I asked my mom for five dollars and handed it to one of them. The man said "Thank you, God bless your soul" and it made his day. It made me feel really good to know I helped someone else out who was in need.

*Brooke, age 14*

# From Me, To You

While reading The Lowell Sun I saw the remains of the burned down apartment complex. The picture was scary. There were children without homes, toys and some had even lost their parents. We found out that The Lowell Wish Project was collecting donations for the fire victims. We called and asked how many children were affected by the fire. I decided to take care of the 3 boys and my sister decided to take care of the 4 girls. I was able to put together care packages with games, Hot Wheels cars and books for the boys. I was very excited to bring the donations to the Wish Project. My sister had finished her packages for the girls. She had picked out books, cards and games for each girl. We arrived at The Wish Project with our donations and a card for the kids wishing them to find some joy in the toys!

*Alexander and Elizabeth, age 8*

*Clara, age 6*

# Strength From Within

I volunteered at a football practice for kids in grades five to eight. There was one individual that stood out to me. This kid was the hardest working one on the team and it was noticeable that he had potential. The last drills were saved for tackling and stances. He was up against the strongest on the team. I pulled him to the side and told him a little tip about tackling in a game. The only way he would do it, was if he could practice by tackling me. I had no pads but I did not care. I agreed to his terms. The coach blows the whistle and I braced myself. After he got up from tackling me, he gave me a huge hug and told me I was awesome. Then he was up against his real opponent, and he was victorious! Practice ended and he had a million questions. He thanked me very much and so did his father. It felt so good knowing I helped!

*Prit, age 12*

Maeve, age 13

# What Goes Around, Comes Around

It was April vacation and my family and I had just returned from a trip to Europe; we were in Logan Airport in Boston. We were waiting to get our luggage off the carrier belt when I saw a mother say to her young boy, "I have to go meet Dad; can you get our luggage off the belt when it comes around?" The boy nodded and his mother left. I was waiting for my own luggage when I saw this same boy struggling with a large black suitcase on the belt; my suitcase was right behind his. I ran over and helped the boy lift his suitcase off the belt and wheeled it to the side for him, leaving my suitcase to pass back around the belt again. I waited with the boy until his mother came back over with his father and they thanked me for helping their son with the baggage.

*Natalie, age 12*

Elizabeth, age 6

# Just What the Doctor Ordered

I was at MGH as a patient.  I wasn't feeling well but enjoyed the aquarium that was in the room.  There was a mother with 3 children.  The oldest was going to be taken in for an emergency surgery early that morning.  The other 2 children were complaining to their mom that they were hungry.  The mom who did not speak much English asked the nurse for food.  The nurse was explaining that her son could not eat as he was to have surgery.  After an hour or so the children were still complaining so I asked my mommy to please go to the cafeteria and buy them food.  My mom went down and got them milk, yogurt and pizza.  When she came back I gave it to them.  I also had one piece of pizza. The little boy came back over to thank me then asked, "Are you going to eat that?" I willingly gave him my piece as well.

*Sophia, age 7*

## Saluting our Soldiers

I was shopping with my mom at the grocery store, like we do every week. This week was a little different though. While we are going through the aisles I noticed a man, dressed as a solider. I told my mom I thought he was really brave for what he does. I asked my mom if we could thank him for his bravery. We went and purchased a gift card for the grocery store. We found him again down the bread aisle. I went up to him and gave the gift card and told him Thank you for being so brave.

*Noel, age 7*

# Love to Keep You Warm

Back in 2010 the tragedy of the Haiti Earthquakes was a big, talked-about thing. At the time, I was a part of a Girl Scout troop, and I remember discussing the earthquakes with my troop. So many people lost everything they had, so my friends and I in the troop decided we wanted to help. We got together and made close to 50 blankets which our troop leader then gave them to her friend who was going on a mission trip to Haiti. Along with the blankets we included cards and other little things that were delivered to many people in need.

*Lily, age 11*

# Helping Hands by the Seashore

I saw this woman with her 2 kids today at the beach. They had to have been less than five years old. She was carrying a lunch box, an umbrella and bunch of other beach stuff. One of the little boys was crying a ton and the other one wasn't cooperating at all. I could tell she was having a hard time keeping track of the boys and carrying all her stuff. She had put her stuff down to pick up her son, when I walked over and asked her if she needed help. She kept saying it was okay but it was obvious she needed the help so I insisted. I helped her take all the things to her car and load the boys in.

*Jade, age 12*

# Canine Compassion

I walked 10 dogs at Greyhound and Friends (dog shelter). I love dogs and I love to be around dogs and that's why I volunteered. I felt really good helping them because some shelter dogs don't have good lives with loving and caring homes. After I walked the dogs it felt good to know that I helped an animal in need. I look forward to going back to greyhounds and friends to help and walk as many dogs as possible! Someday you should go to shelter dogs and cats in need and after you will feel just amazing!

*Clare, age 10*

# Call of the Wild

I have loved wolves for my whole life. Last year I found out about a cool place called Wolf Hollow that houses wolves of all ages. I adopted (sponsored) a wolf to help raise money for his food and care. I am very happy that I could help the wolves. I am hoping to help and sponsor wolves in the future!

*Clara, age 12*

*Elizabeth, age 6*

## Paper or Plastic

One afternoon after coming out of the grocery store, I saw a lady struggling to put her groceries in her car. So, I went up to her and asked if I could help and she said, "Yes". So I helped her put them in her car and she thanked me. I felt very helpful after what I had done and it made me realize that being kind to people can really make someone's day!

*Priscilla, age 9*

Maeve, age 13

# Locks of Love

I recently donated ten inches of my hair to Locks of Love and Children with Hair Loss. Both of these organizations take donated hair and create wigs for children who suffer from illnesses and injuries that cause them to lose their hair. This past summer I donated ten inches. I choose to donate because the wigs help give these kids, who are already going through so much, a little more confidence. The first time I donated was in 5th grade. I not really sure what got me interested in doing this, but it was such an amazing feeling! Three years later I cut my hair again in the eighth grade. This past time will definitely not be my last!

*Megan, age 14*

# Running On Inspiration

My family is associated with the American Liver Foundation through my younger brother. Each year they have athletes that run in the Boston Marathon to raise money for the foundation. The runners are paired up with patients that have liver diseases such as Biliary Atresia. The foundation is a great program and it helps patients and their families meet and connect. It is also perfect for the runners to get inspired and learn about why they run for the liver team. Throughout the course of the marathon training season my family and I participate by setting up and running water stations during their training runs. We spend time getting to know the runners, patients, and other volunteers throughout the season. It's a great experience to watch the runners and be a part of helping such a great cause.

*Madison, age 11*

## Sometimes it's So Simple

I remember once I was grocery shopping with my mom. We were in an aisle and an elderly lady was in the same aisle as us. This woman accidently knocked down a bunch of boxes. She was having difficulty bending down to pick all the boxes up so, I decided to help her out. I leaned down and picked all the boxes up and put them back on the shelf. When I stood back up, the women looked so thankful that I helped her. To me it was just a simple task but, to her it was a kind stranger doing something for her that she wasn't able to.

*Lauren, age 11*

# Camp Kindness

This summer I volunteered my time as a camp counselor. This camp was created for underprivileged children aged 6-12. I heard from many of the campers that I was their favorite, and that made me very proud that I made a connection with the kids. I played games with the campers in the playground, read them books during reading time, made comic books at the art table, and even brought in my guitar to entertain and share with some who could never afford to buy a guitar. The experience was very enlightening, coming from a very "well off" and homogeneous town, I had the opportunity to learn about the lives of wonderful kids who didn't get all the opportunities I did, and I tried my best to make their personal experiences at the camp memorable and enjoyable.

*Jacob, age 12*

## Positive Pen Pal

I went into school early and left little notes for my teachers, the school nurse and my guidance counselor to find all over the classrooms/their offices - the notes just said positive quotes and reasons why they are great people. It was fun to watch some of my teachers find the notes and smile - they never found out it was me!

*Jamnah, age 12*

*Morey School First Grade*

# Happy Valentine's Day

My friend's brother, Richie, is at the Naval Academy. When he graduates he is going to be an officer in the navy. Right now he is working on his college degree while doing navy training. This year on Valentine's Day my friends and I decided to make cards and bake cookies to send to him so that he could share with his friends. We wanted him to know that we appreciate his dedication to serve our country. My friend was thrilled and she helped us bake the cookies. My mother helped us send the package.

*Lauren, age 11*

# Reese's For a Smile

When we were in line at the grocery store, I asked the cashier what her favorite candy bar was. She said it was Reese's Peanut Butter Cups. I went over to where the candy was and grabbed a package and put it on the belt. The cashier laughed and said is this for you? I said no it's for YOU! My mom told her that we'd like to buy the candy bar for her to keep and enjoy!

*Jax, age 6*

# Stories Shared with Friends

# Class Clowns

When I was in 6th grade, I had one really close friend in my homeroom. In the middle of the year, she got sick, and she had to miss a few months of school. I decided to ask my teacher if we could, make videos from our class to cheer her up! All of my classmates were excited about participating, and we ended up making about 5 videos! We choreographed dances, sang songs, and just reminded our friend how much we missed her. When she watched the videos, she was happy that we were thinking about her, and the videos made her laugh. I was happy that I could make her smile and that made a difference in my life.

*Olivia, age 11*

# Thank You for Being a Friend

Last year a new student came to my school and she was disabled. She was all alone and no one would help her out other than the teachers. I felt she needed a friend, because everyone deserves a friend and she was sitting all alone. I walked over to her and introduced myself. She smiled when I did, and seemed really happy to have another kid to talk to. I helped her for a couple days, showing her where her classes were, sitting with her and trying to get to know her. I did this until she got a teacher assigned to her permanently so she no longer needed me to show her where classes were. Now, although I don't see her as much, I always smile at her and say, "Hi!" when I do.

*Sarah, age 13*

*Brody, age 6*

# The Chain Gang

My friend and I went to Kimball farms in Westford. As we were waiting in line to go on the bumper boats, we saw four kids in line behind us. I decided to buy four tickets. My friend and I handed one to each of the four kids. The adults told them that they had to pay us back but we told them all about doing acts of kindness for other people. They seemed interested and began to think of ways that they could pass on these generous acts. They thanked us very much and enjoyed the ride. Later that day we saw those kids in line for ice-cream and we watched them pay for ice cream for a family of three. One of the boys looked over at us and smiled. The family seemed very thankful for this kind gesture and went on their way with their ice-creams. My friend and I had no idea that one small act could start a chain reaction.

*Ryan, age 12*

# Brave Ava

I decided to make a care package to send a Kindergartener from North Salem Elementary School in Salem, NH. She was diagnosed with a rare brain tumor over the winter and had surgery to remove the tumor that was the size of a baseball. Originally she was at Dana Farber & Children's Hospital in Boston, but moved to Cleveland Clinic Children's for further treatment. She is currently having chemo and has more surgeries ahead before she will be better. Although she has a long road ahead, she is BRAVE. I sent Ava a basket with books, a stuffed animal, snacks, a journal and coloring books to help put her mind at ease when she needs it. The 5$^{th}$ grade class made a video to make Ava smile and know that she has many friends at North Salem Elementary School cheering for her to have a full recovery.

*Anthony, age 10*

# Unexpected Lunchtime Encounter

One day I was in school at lunch and I was sitting with my friends. As I was eating, I saw this girl sitting alone and I mentioned her to my friends. They didn't seem to care, but I decided no one should ever have to sit alone at lunch. I got up, telling my friends I was going to go sit with her. I asked if I could sit down and the biggest smile spread across her face. We talked all lunch and she ended up being really cool. We now sit together all the time and we're good friends. Random Acts of Kindness can lead to amazing friendships and happiness!

*Erin, age 9*

# A+ Effort

I went back to school shopping for school supplies with my mom and my little brother. We picked up some crayons, markers, pencils, colored pencils and pencil sharpeners to donate for 20 kids. They were dropped off at the Boys & Girls Club of Greater Salem. I am part of the after school program during the school year and attend camp a few weeks in the summer too. It was fun to shop for me, but also fun to pick things for others.

*Anthony, age 10*

# All It Takes Is Kindness

Last year, one of my friends lost her uncle, who she was very close to. This girl and I weren't best friends, but we sat together at lunch. I did my best to make her laugh and smile, since I could tell how hard of a time she was having. Recently, she and I have gotten closer, and one day, my mom received an email from this girl's mom. To paraphrase, her mom thanked me for being there for my friend. She had been mildly depressed, and just my small effort of trying to make her laugh and being there for her made a huge difference. Moral of the story, no matter how small it seems, no act of kindness goes unnoticed.

*Caitlin, age 12*

Maeve, age 13

# Ready, Set, Inspire

One day this summer I was at volleyball camp and in the morning session we all played and competed against each other in drills. Later on that day they put us in teams based it on our ability and how well we play! All the teams scrimmaged and then the top two teams scrimmaged against each other to see who won first place. One team (I have to say) was not as great at volleyball, they were very young. The other team was pretty good! The coaches told everyone to sit on the side of who you think will win! Literally everyone sat on the side of the team that was pretty good, but I sat on the side of the team that didn't look like they could win! I cheered them on and on and they actually won!

*Brooke, age 12*

## Kindness Swap

When I was at the book swap, I picked out a pop-up book. As I walked away, my friend Emily asked, "Can I have the pop-up book"? I told her, "Yes"! Emily was happy she got the book and I was happy because I made her happy!

*Kaylene, age 6*

# Walk This Way

I walk to the Boys and Girls Club after school every day. There is a group of us about 10-20 kids that do this; the same kids every day. Usually I walk with my sister and a couple friends. The other day I asked another girl if she wanted to walk with us. She is new to school and usually walks by herself. No one likes to walk alone and I think this girl really appreciated it. Later at the Boys and Girls Club she played foosball with us. I am happy that I made a new friend and she is happy she knows more people.

*Laura, age 10*

# Buddy Bench

At school we have a buddy bench. A buddy bench is a bench a child can sit on if they feel lonely at recess. Last year a girl in the 2nd grade sat on the bench. Her name is Christine. I went over and asked her if she wanted to play foursquare with me and my friends. Every day since the day she sat on the buddy bench, she plays four square with us. I am happy because I made a new friend. But more importantly I made Christine's day! She has never felt lonely at recess again!

*Kimmie, age 9*

# Baking Up a Thank You

My soccer coach is someone who I really look up to. He really cares about our team, giving us advice and motivating us to be the best players (and people) we can be. My team and I got together to think of someway to say thank you for all he does, something he would really appreciate. We made a "funfetti" cake and decorated it with a big THANK YOU and made a giant card that everyone signed. He was speechless when we brought it to practice! It wasn't the end of the season or for any particular reason - we just wanted him to know how much we appreciate him. I think he really liked it.

*Amelia, age 10*

# Mint to Be Friends

In my middle school you can send a candy cane to someone during Christmas time. A lot of the times you send them to your friends and say Merry Christmas! But last year I decided to send a couple to a quiet girl in my class. She and I talked sometimes but I noticed she did not talk to many people. I thought it would be a nice surprise for her. On the day that the candy canes were delivered she was so happy to get some! She thanked me, and we have continued talking every day in class.

*Zoe, age 12*

Maeve, age 13

# A Kind Equation

In 7th grade, I realized a lot of people asked me for help with math homework. I decided to create a math chat on Skype containing all the students in our math level. If you needed help or had a question, you could ask it in the math chat. At first I was still the only one answering questions, but once people started using the chat frequently help got out fast. Everybody could chime in to help solve a problem, and although I was still the go-to guy for questions, it became much more enjoyable. The chat continued into 8th grade and eventually evolved to include help for all topics. Answers started coming from a variety of people. It was a fun place to get help and just socialize in general (we went off topic way too often)

*Jason, age 12*

Maeve, age 13

# Education Appreciation

This past year it was one of my favorite teacher's birthdays. My friend and I wanted to show our appreciation for him because he always does so much for us students. We brain stormed ideas and eventually decided on making a big book of reasons why everyone appreciated him. We asked almost a hundred people their best memory with him and why they were thankful for him. We wrote them all down in a nice book with pictures. When we gave it to him he was so happy and said it was the best present he had ever received! It felt really good to do something for someone who always does things for me!

*Haley, age 13*

## Sending Comfort

My best friend was moving. Both of us were extremely sad about this. She was staying in the same town but she is no longer a bike ride away. Knowing how upset she was, I made a basket for her. It was a new home survival kit, with all her favorite things! I put in her favorite candy, (butterfingers), her favorite magazine, a sketch book and a new set of colored pencils. She loves drawing and I thought it might help her become comfortable with the new house!

*Lexi, age 7*

Want some ideas to start your own Random Acts of Kindness?

- Dollar bills or bags of change taped to the vending machines.

- Donate toys to the sandbox at the playground, burying "treasure" in the sand at a playground.

- Leave treats and messages for the mail carrier in the mailbox. Leave the flag up so he thinks he is picking up mail, but it really is a surprise for him!

- Buy coloring books and crayons and put them in Ziploc bags and bring them to your local emergency room.

- Cut out a bunch of heart shapes and write and draw on them. Then stick them inside a book and returned it to the library for someone to find.

- Be a good neighbor! Bring over a flower or baked good and help with a household chore!

- Slip paper hearts that say "It's Random Acts of Kindness Day! Have a great day! Pass it on!" under the windshield wipers of parked cars.

- Have a clean-up party at your favorite playground.

- Write notes of appreciation and bring flowers or goodies to teachers or other important people, such as the principal, nurse, custodian, and secretary of your school.

- Recycle cans and use reusable shopping bags.

- Make a bird feeder.

- Help your parents by taking out the trash or doing some yard work without taking an allowance.

- Donate your old toys to someone that does not have as many as you.

- Go to church without making a fuss.

- Make a home-made card to say Thank You to someone special.

- Help carry the groceries into the house.

# With Our Thanks and Gratitude

Inspire to Act for Kids was written for kids by kids. It is a collection of wonderful short stories of the kind acts kids can do when they are encouraged to live an attitude of gratitude. Each of the stories and illustrations in this book were selected from the many stories we received or acts of kindness we witnessed.

To help us, we hired high school summer intern's to collect the stories and work with local schools, youth groups and YMCA's to interview kids and ask them to share their random acts of kindness.

We would like to extend our heartfelt appreciation and gratitude to our interns and young artists, Kelly Gaunya, Maeve Cross, Sarah Dockman and Elizabeth Kurth as well as our graphic artist, Stacy Bennett.

In addition, we partnered with Anne Conant, an amazing first grade teacher at Morey School. Her passion for teaching an attitude of gratitude with young kids is inspiring.

Finally, a very special thank you to Jessica Boisvert, Shaina Bendzewicz and Colleen Nagri for their help and assistance. Their collaborative dedication and support made this book possible.